This WALKER
book belongs to:

by **Katrina Germein**

illustrated by

Tom Jellett

WALKER BOOKS
AND SUBSIDIARIES
LONDON · BOSTON · SYDNEY · AUCKLAND

My dad
STILL
thinks he's
funny

My dad thinks
he's really funny.

I say, "What's the time?"
and Dad says,

"Time to get a watch."

I say, "I'm tired," and Dad says, "Tired of what?"

I say, "I'm bored," and Dad says,

"A surfboard or a floorboard?"

My dad thinks he's really funny.

Grandpa tells me I've grown a foot.
Dad says, "How many has he got now?"

Mum tells me I get my brains from her.
Dad says, "I've still got mine."

When Gran tells me there's something special about me, Dad says, "Yeah, that's his father."

My dad thinks he's really funny.

I suggest chicken. Dad says, "That's fowl."
Mum suggests lamb.
Dad says, "No shanks."

My dad thinks
he's really
funny.

I say I feel like a milkshake and Dad says, "You don't look like one."

When we have pizza,
Dad says,
"Cut mine in
four pieces.
I'm too full
for eight."

My dad
thinks he's
really funny.

When there's cake, Dad says, "Who's the bully who whipped the cream? They probably beat the eggs as well."

And when there are candles, Dad says, "Don't worry. I've got the hose!"

My dad thinks he's really funny.

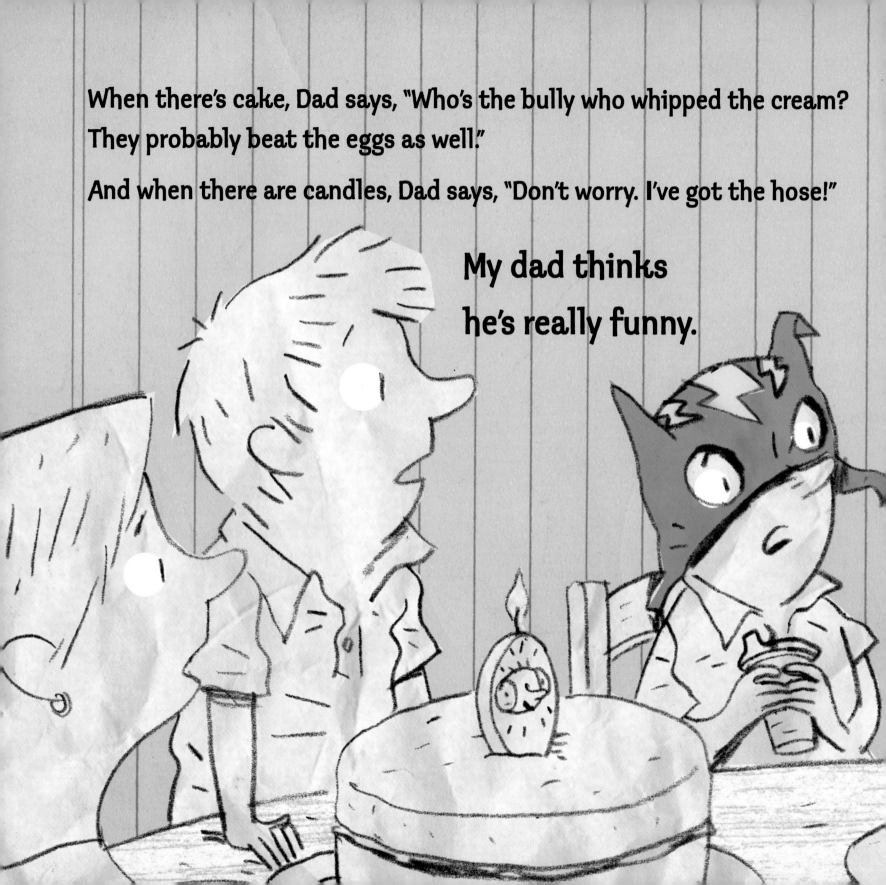

Mum says we can have the juice in the fridge and Dad says,

"I can't fit in there!"

Grandpa says that Mum's in the toilet
and Dad says, "Quick! Pull her out!"

My dad thinks he's really funny.

If I ask Dad to put my shoes on, he says, "They won't fit me."

If I tell Dad I've lost a shoe, he says, "You'll have to hop."

If I tell Dad I need new shoes, he says,
"But those ones were new when we bought them."

My dad thinks he's really funny.

Gran says, "Where have you been?"

Dad says, "I haven't been anywhere. I prefer peas."

I say that no one can ride my bike and Dad says, "No one's not here, so I'll have her turn."

My dad thinks he's really funny.

Mum suggests we take the short cut home.
Dad says, "But my hair is fine."

I ask for a hand
and Dad starts
clapping.

"Dad," I say, "that joke's so weak it's almost a fortnight."

And I think I'm quite funny too.

First published by **black dog books**

This edition published 2015 by Walker Books Ltd
87 Vauxhall Walk, London SE11 5HJ

10 9 8 7 6 5 4 3 2 1

This book has been typeset in Klepto

Printed in China

British Library Cataloguing in Publication Data:
a catalogue record for this book
is available from the British Library

iSBN 978-1-4063-6055-4

www.walker.co.uk

With lots of love for Billy,
Riley, Eddie and Ellie, and
their funny parents, Benny
and Jacci. KG

For Harry, Ben and Jack. TJ

KATRINA GERMEIN is an award-winning picture-book author whose other titles include *My Dad Thinks He's Funny* and *My Mum Says the Silliest Things*. Katrina, who works part-time as a teacher, lives in Adelaide, Australia, with her husband, their three children and an energetic dog named Mango.

TOM JELLETT is an illustrator whose work has appeared in a number of books – including *My Dad Thinks He's Funny* and *My Mum Says the Silliest Things* – as well as in national newspapers such as *The Australian* and the *Daily Telegraph*. Tom lives in Sydney, Australia.

Look out for:

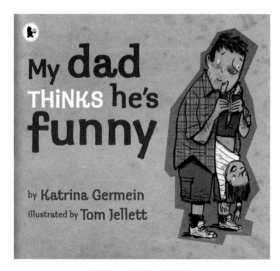

978-1-4063-4730-2

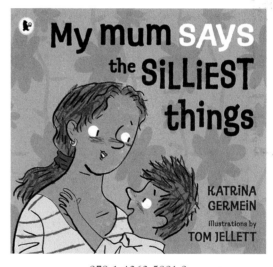

978-1-4063-5891-9

Available from all good booksellers

www.walker.co.uk